Littlehampton GHOST TOUR

A self-guided walk around Littlehampton town centre

ISBN 978-1-9998644-2-2

A CHINDI production
Cover by Christine Hammacott of The Art of Communication
All other images supplied by Rosemary Noble, Angela Petch and Patricia Feinberg Stoner

This book was prepared for publication by Heather Robbins.

Thanks to the people of Littlehampton for sharing their stories, especially Ellie Boiling of the Dolphin; Ivor Holland of Quality Textiles
and Tyndall James for his knowledge of Littlehampton history.

CONTENTS

Part I – The Tour. 1

Part II – Ghost Stories 21

I Footprints by Albert Roy. 23

II Moonlight by Patricia Feinberg Stoner. 26

III River of Destiny by Janet Edington 28

IV The Ghost of Oyster Pond by Philippa Bower 31

V The Harbour Cat by Teresa Harrison-Best. 32

VI Bingo by Carol Thomas 34

VII Littlehampton Lily by Maureen Wells. 36

VIII Supermarket Challenge by Angela Petch 38

IX A Halloween Story by Maggie Brown 41

X Maud Gray by Annette Brampton 43

XI Flyers by Rosemary Noble. 45

WELCOME TO
LITTLEHAMPTON

PART I

THE GHOST TOUR

Welcome

Thank you for choosing to take our tour around the ancient harbour town of Littlehampton. There are lots of ghosts to discover as well as snippets of history to divert you along the way. If that weren't enough, we invited writing groups around Littlehampton to submit ghost stories based on the culture and history of this much-loved seaside resort and we include some of the stories in Part II. Enjoy your walk and we hope your dreams are not too disturbed by the spooky tales from this book.

1. PANAMA JOE'S, ARCADE ROAD

We're going to begin at Panama Joe's, a good place to refresh yourself with a glass of something before you start. Joe, the genial owner of Panama Joe's Latin American restaurant, is no stranger to spirits. 'I used to see a lady all in white at a previous restaurant I owned,' he recalls.

On the other hand, rumours that the courtyard behind Panama Joe's is haunted are a surprise to him: the only ghost he has seen is in the restaurant itself. 'I used to sleep here sometimes when we were doing up the place, and I would see a small kid. I often see him now, sometimes in the restaurant and sometimes in the bar.'

Joe is friendly to ghosts: he calls them 'cool', which is perhaps why this particular haunting is benign.

Walk past Evans Garden Courtyard towards the Arcade. This is where they used to stable working horses. Some say you can hear the sound of a girl giggling in the yard when no children are to be seen. Walk through the Arcade, maybe stop to read the ghost story, Littlehampton Lily (page 36), on your way through. Turn left and head right across the road.

2. AHEAD TOE, EAST STREET

It's a long-established and well-liked beauty salon, but that's not all: there are ghostly goings-on at Ahead Toe, as the owner, Celia Thomson, knows all too well.

Children are often heard running around and shouting when there is no-one there. A mirror vibrates on the wall with no apparent cause, and on more than one occasion a couch in one of the rooms has been inexplicably pushed against the wall and the contents of a cupboard flung across the room. There is one room, Celia reports, which children refuse to enter because it has such a spooky aura.

She also recalls an encounter with a man in a mustard-coloured suit. 'We were redecorating, and I was doing some painting on the top landing,' Celia recalls. 'I became aware of a man standing behind me: he'd somehow come up two flights of stairs without my hearing him. I turned to ask him to wait for a moment, but there was no-one there. I got a strong feeling he wasn't a very nice man.'

The salon is on the first floor of the building, and its terrace garden has seen its fair share of hauntings too. Vilma Lazareviciene owns the Black Swan hairdresser whose back room is directly beneath the terrace. She remembers hearing someone walking overhead wearing stiletto heels and dragging pots across the terrace. When she reported what she thought were intruders, Celia told her that the salon was closed that day, and no-one was there.

Vilma now has a picture, given to her by Celia, which both women believe helps to restore peace. It's an ordinary, rather sentimental picture of two children by a fireside, in a heavy black frame. 'It was given to me by a white witch,' Celia says, 'and when Vilma moved in downstairs I passed it on to her.'

No-one knows exactly who might be haunting Ahead Toe, but there may be a clue in its location. It's said that long ago there was a pond opposite where the salon stands, where women accused of witchcraft were ducked to prove their guilt or innocence. Guilty or innocent, the poor women perished: either by drowning or by fire.

3. THE SPOTTED COW (NOW THE FISH FACTORY)

Next door to Ahead Toe used to be the Spotted Cow, now a reputable fish restaurant. This may at one time have been a Tannery. LIGHT (Littlehampton Investigative Ghost Hunting Team) did a séance here before the pub closed, and it appeared to be haunted by a man called George. He is a very dark character and comes with a deep sense of foreboding as well as mist and a putrid smell. At one point, he was asked to make himself known and a phone camera clicked with no one near it. The photograph (seen by the editor) shows a man's head and shoulders in the background but in outline shape only.

4. THE GREEN LADY

Further up East Street, past the convent, you can see a blue plaque high up on the wall. If you venture down the twitten at the side of The Green Lady Hostel, will you catch a glimpse of the lady in the green dress? She is reputed to wander the alleyway in search of someone or something. Beware when darkness falls.

The Green Lady Hostel, established in 1900, was supported by a remarkable lady called Mary Neal (1860 – 1944) who came to live in Littlehampton between 1922 and 1940 at Green Bushes, Flora Road. She was a suffragist, social reformer, Justice of the Peace and folk-dance revivalist. In her twenties, she joined the West London Methodist Mission working with vulnerable people. She established a club for working women and in 1895 set up the Esperance Club to improve the lives of impoverished young women by employing them as dressmakers with good wages and set working hours. This was known as Maison Esperance. The Green Lady Hostel in Littlehampton opened in 1900 and welcomed women of all ages, means and denominations for holidays by the sea. It was purchased on a mortgage in the names of the Hon. Lily Montagu, a famous philanthropist, and Miss Emmeline Pethick, suffragette and close friend of Mary, housing up to sixty girls for a fortnight.

In this centenary year of the first votes for women, it is fitting to remember this special lady and her involvement with the suffragette movement. Although not very active herself, she wrote regularly for "The Suffragette" newspaper and concentrated on the Esperance movement to spread the notion that women deserved more legal rights.

The question is, who is the lady in the green dress? One of the poor guests or Mary herself, her spirit restless in a world that remains unfair?

Head back down to the town and turn right into the High Street.

5. THE CROWN

Although smugglers' tunnels linked the Crown to the Dolphin and the White Hart, the current manager has no knowledge of less earth-bound spirits inhabiting this establishment. However, in the course of our research, we talked to an ex-employee who distinctly heard tapping on the back door at closing time, but no one was there, and the noise of people moving upstairs. A current barmaid reports seeing, on a CCTV monitor, orbs of light dancing around the back door. Once, as she turned off the lights at closing time, a tray from under the counter threw itself across the bar, hitting the chilled drinks cabinet on the other side. Could this be the smuggler boy, Billy, who was crushed in the tunnel between The Crown and the Dolphin? Billy haunts the Dolphin too.

You could take a break at the Crown or Dolphin for a drink and read the ghost story, Flyers, on page 45 or a Halloween Story on page 41.

6. THE DOLPHIN - THE MOST HAUNTED PUB IN LITTLEHAMPTON

Although rebuilt during the early twentieth century, the hauntings continue. A pub of this name has been on this site since 1736. It was built over a dried river bed, possibly the original path of the Arun, before a new cut was made in the early 1700s. Some say that when the cut was made, a Saxon cemetery was disturbed and since then Surrey Street has experienced several hauntings. If that were the case, one would expect the hauntings to be Saxon in nature, but they mostly appear to be Victorian.

Lord Byron stayed here for a few days in 1806 – see section 16 for more about Lord Byron's stay in Littlehampton. Could he have stayed here because he liked to experience life amongst ordinary people?

The Dolphin has the largest and deepest cellars of the three connected pubs and was used, not only by smugglers, but also as a mortuary for the victims of World War Two bombings in Pier Road, when a row of houses was flattened, inflicting many casualties.

Its claim as the most haunted pub in Littlehampton is much vaunted by Ellie Boiling, the landlady. The pub is the subject of an hour-long film on Really TV called My House is Haunted, broadcast in 2018.

The Dolphin has at least four ghosts. Little Dolly (real name, Ada Constance) died of diphtheria as a child in the pub and has left her mark on a piece of cloth in an upstairs room. An image of a child can clearly be seen on it. There are also William and his niece Jane, who was the cook. Jane haunts the toilet following her murder by her uncle. Finally, there's Little Billy, the smuggler's boy, who also haunts The Crown.

If you have time, or on a further visit, you could head north for more hauntings. Or turn left now into Surrey Street and jump to section 10 in your book.

7. THE LOCOMOTIVE, TERMINUS ROAD, BY THE STATION

Before this pub closed in 2007 and was later demolished, a group of people gathered to say goodbye. A prayer was offered at some point in the proceedings. Shortly afterwards, everyone heard the music from a barrel organ start up, the chattering of many voices and a bell sounding time at the bar. There were upwards of fifteen people there at the time who witnessed it. Do not confuse this with the Locomotive in Lyminster.

8. THE STEAM PACKET, RIVER ROAD

For more than 150 years The Steam Packet pub has stood on River Road, Littlehampton, just by the historic footbridge across the Arun. The pub was named after the steam boat service that ran from Littlehampton to Honfleur, in Normandy, from 1863 to 1882.

The Steam Packet was closed for almost five years for refurbishment and reopened in June 2013. However, that hasn't deterred any resident ghosts, as landlady Arletta and barman Chris can testify. Arletta recalls: 'My husband bought the pub in 2009, and I came over from Poland to live here in 2013. Yes, there is a ghost: a lady. A friend told me about her, but at first I didn't believe it. Then I sensed her presence, and now often if I sit up late by the fire I know she's there and I chat to her. She's not hostile or scary, in fact I think she likes me.'

Chris recalls the time when he saw another ghost. 'I was alone in the pub: the chef had gone home, or so I thought. Then I saw a man standing in the doorway of the kitchen. When I looked again, he had gone. I asked the chef next day if he had come back for any reason, but he hadn't.'

Apart from ghostly apparitions, the pub radio also appears to be haunted: it turns itself on every day at 12 noon, even when it has no batteries in it. Anyone keen to know what station the ghost listens to, though, will be disappointed: it seems only static can be heard.

Chris also has a scary tale to tell about Wellesley Court in Fitzalan Road. 'We used to live in the bottom flat. One day I took a picture of my Mum on my phone, and when we looked at it there was the blacked-out figure of a baby in her arms. We also used to hear knocking on the windows when there was no-one there.'

9. A HOUSE IN RIVER ROAD

John Burtenshaw has memories of a house in River Road which 'was in our family for as long as I can remember.'

He recalls a presence he felt a number of times while he lived there. 'One of the builders said he felt something behind him; he never returned. There were sudden temperature drops, and I heard footsteps when only I was there. My father also experienced it when he was visiting.'

Turn left at this handsome square to return to Surrey Street.

10. QUALITY TEXTILES

Who would expect this tiny, unassuming shop to be riddled with ghosts? The owner, Ivor Holland, was utterly sceptical until he experienced them himself but is now so convinced that he has become a spiritual medium.

Firstly, there is William Dyer, a tailor, who owned the shop back in the nineteenth century. William likes to play tricks by hurling stock around or sounding a buzzer when the shop is locked and the owner is climbing the outside fire escape. It is always when the third step is reached that the buzzer sounds. Sometimes he just likes to check up on people when they visit the bathroom. A black head and hands appear around the corner. William can be identified by the scent of wintergreen which he applies to his sore ankles.

Then there's William's wife who wears a flowery scent and is dressed in grey as she travels through the shop. Or granddaughter Annabel, with long blond hair and giggling smile. She blamed herself for her parents' death in a house fire, a few doors away, until she was released back into the spirit world, her mind at rest. The owner still experiences her presence.

What about the tiny workhouse boy, locked in a gloomy, upstairs cupboard for not working hard enough, a single, guttering candle playing havoc with his asthma? Or finally, the young man locked in an attic, away from prying eyes for being both simple and displaying an interest in young men. It is said that any woman poking her head into his world is immediately smitten by a migraine.

The property, owned by William Dyer, a wealthy and influential man in his time, extended into what is now Iceland, but used to be Woolworths. People would hear noises in the upstairs stockroom so maybe the ghosts still travel between the properties.

11. ART AND CRAFT GALLERY, SURREY STREET

Walk to the gallery on the corner. It used to be The Offie until recently. The new owner was unaware of anything creepy in his cellar when we talked to him, but we have been reliably informed of strange goings-on down there.

There was a chair stored in the cellar reputed to bring bad luck and the previous tenants refused to touch it, let alone sit on it. Frequent sightings have also occurred of an angry man, either at the top or the bottom of these cellar stairs. Originally the premises were a pub. Apparently, the wife of the owner of Littlehampton dairy was conducting an affair in the pub with a ship's captain. (The dairy used to be opposite the council offices.) The dairy owner surprised the lovers at the pub and challenged the captain to a fight and the sea captain died. Whether the angry spirit is that of the dairy manager or the sea captain, we will leave to your imaginations.

Maybe somebody should warn the new owner not to sit on the chair in his cellar.

Carefully cross the road to the pub opposite; watch for cars travelling around the bend.

12. THE WHITE HART, SURREY STREET

Back in the 1700s, this pub was the first Dolphin on Surrey Street. After an argument, the landlord's brother opened a second pub called the Dolphin, which is now on the corner of Surrey Street and High Street. This original Dolphin has changed its name several times over the centuries. It may have been the White Swan, which led to the Cob and Pen, before becoming the White Hart.

Although the current manager knows of no ghosts, a previous landlord of a generation ago said it was haunted by a female ghost, a maid who died in a fire in the upper rooms. She used to haunt the stairs in the upper part of the building.

This was one of the three pubs joined by smugglers' tunnels. In the present bar, you can see a capped-off glass opening to the well and tunnels. All the tunnels have been blocked off, but wouldn't it be a huge tourist attraction if they could be reopened and guided tours arranged?

Head down towards the harbour past the handsome former captains' and ship-builders' houses and attractive square. Stand by the Sea Life Centre and look north towards the Marina, beyond the footbridge.

13. THE SEAHORSE RESTAURANT, THE MARINA

There used to be a floating restaurant in the marina. Originally the Hygea was a Port of London Barge until it was retired in the 1970s and in its early days it may have been a hospital ship. It was bought and renamed the Seahorse, opening as a floating restaurant and pub in Littlehampton in July 1984. Soon after, the haunting began. A night watchman was the first to experience it. On a hot muggy night, he began to feel a cold draught, then a terror that made his hair stand on end. It lasted for ninety minutes before returning to normal. Others heard doors banging, saw moving shadows or witnessed hanging pot plants swaying in the bar.

Bill Hunter, a former fisherman, recalls: 'Some of us who worked as night watchmen for the marina used to stay on board. To say it was scary was an understatement: voices were heard and there were footsteps up and down passages. We didn't like it at all, but it was warmer on board than outside.'

The restaurant sank after a few years. Do you remember it?

Head south along the harbour path; stop to read the boards showing the fascinating history of the harbour. Sit down and close your eyes and listen to the sounds of yesteryear, the sound of ship building, of fishermen catching the tide and unloading their catches. Or imagine the nights without a moon when smugglers would silently go about their business.

14. SMUGGLERS IN LITTLEHAMPTON

Smuggling in the 18th and 19th centuries was common practice, a black economy that played a major role in everyday life, employing more than 40,000 people. The smugglers of Kent and Sussex were the leaders in the field and it is no surprise that Littlehampton, with its gently sloping shoreline, was an active smuggling centre. Free from rocky headlands, it was easy to load and unload shallow boats and smuggle goods across the Downs or up the river Arun and on to London via the Wey and Arun Canal that linked to the Thames. Customs records from 1736 show that 229 smuggling boats were confiscated on the Sussex coast, with 200,000 gallons of brandy seized. Two thousand smugglers were prosecuted, and the consequences were transportation to colonies, compulsory naval service, or imprisonment.

Littlehampton was a safe haven for smugglers, with pubs linking to the riverside via tunnels. They were considered leaders in their field, providing 'brandy for the parson and baccy for the clerk'. Henry Baker, the Supervisor of Customs Officers in Littlehampton in the early 18th century, said that he was 'no more use for this service than a gull on the beach.' It is known that many magistrates were customers of the smugglers and feared retaliation by the smuggling community if they dared to imprison culprits. In order to dissuade the curious public from their illegal activities, stories were invented about ghosts and ghouls, especially near places where booty was stored.

Carry on past Mussel Row where the Oyster fishermen lived and berthed their boats nearby. You might want to tarry at the Oyster Pond.

15. THE OYSTER POND

Take some time out to read a poem, The Ghost of Oyster Pond, page 31 and Maud Gray, page 43.

Look south and imagine the windmill sails turning and Beach House Hotel. This hotel was where people of quality stayed in preference to the town. This is now the site of the funfair.

16. LORD BYRON

Lord Byron, the well-known and infamous poet, visited Littlehampton in 1806, aged eighteen, during his vacation from Trinity College, Cambridge. He was in serious financial difficulties and perhaps that was the reason he stayed at the Dolphin, described by Harry Long, as 'a poor place in a dirty village', rather than the more salubrious Beach House Hotel, near the windmill. Or perhaps it was the fact that the Dolphin was reputed to be haunted which appealed to him. After all, his home, Newstead Abbey, itself is haunted. Witness Byron's poem, The Black Friar. Stanza Four reads:

When an heir is born, he's heard to mourn,
And when aught is to befall
That ancient line, in the pale moonshine
He walks from hall to hall.
His form you may trace, but not his face,
'T is shadow'd by his cowl:
But his eyes may be seen from the folds between,
And they seem of a parted soul.

But not many people know that Byron, although a strong swimmer, almost drowned at Littlehampton. One day, Byron and his friend, Edward Long, jumped off the end of the pier into the river. The strong current swept them out to sea. Harry Long, Edwards's brother, records that they 'were carried such a distance as I could barely discern their heads, popping up and down like ducks upon the sea.' Swimming in an immense semi-circle, against the tide, they managed with difficulty to make it back to shore. If Byron had died, we would not have had such poems as 'She Walks in Beauty, Like the Night' nor the description of him as 'mad, bad and dangerous to know' by Lady Caroline Lamb. Nor would his daughter, Ada Lovelace, famed mathematician and pioneer of computing, have been born.

17. THE FUNFAIR AND THE FORTS

Locals remember the now deceased ghost train did have an actual ghostly presence haunting it. The Funfair was built on the site of the old battery guarding the port from the French. Could it be one of the old soldiers is still at his post, guarding Littlehampton from suspicious visitors? On the opposite side of the harbour stand the ruins of the Fort, built in the 1850s.

If you get the chance, go across the pedestrian bridge to see if you can find them. There's a plan to restore the fort.

There are many stories about soldiers stationed at the battery or the fort getting into trouble while swimming in the harbour. Could one of these drowned soldiers have been the ghost at the funfair?

18. HERE BE DRAGONS

For this final stop you will have to get in your car and drive to Lyminster. Close by the Church of St Mary Magdalene is a deep, round and reputedly bottomless pond known as Knucker's Hole. It is inhabited, legend says, by a knucker – a water dragon. The curious name comes from the Old English *nicor* which means "water monster" and is used in the poem Beowulf.

For years, the Lyminster knucker ravaged the surrounding area until he was slain: either - legends vary - by a brave knight or poisoned by a pie fed to him by a local lad named Jim Pulk.

If you venture inside the church you will find a medieval tombstone next to the font: this marks the last resting place of the dragon slayer, be he brave knight or local lad.

We hope you have enjoyed your tour of the ghostly sights of Littlehampton. You may know of more, in which case, email us at chindibooks@outlook.com – we may be able to include your story if the book goes to a further edition.

PART II

THE GHOST STORIES

1

FOOTPRINTS

Albert Roy

April Fool's Day, five and a half decades ago. And this is true: the footprints appeared overnight. Of course, some took it as a practical joke, but I saw the tracks laid down.

And I saw the ghostly monsters which made them.

Local legend tells of primeval forests submerged off Littlehampton, where ancient creatures stalked before the sea rose to imprison the land. There's even a sunken medieval village out there – Cudlow. True again: divers have found fossilised remnants of roots and tree stumps. At very low tides odd pieces get washed up on the beach.

That night still haunts me.

I was fifteen – randy, raging, and rough around the edges, which is another way of saying I was dumb and thought I knew it all, especially with Anne. I lived over a shopping parade: front bedrooms allowed me to sneak out the back without my parents knowing. Anne's parents lived in a big house on the Beaumont, the first home I knew to have double-glazing. From the garage roof at the side, she could ease down onto a coal bunker and drop softly to the ground.

We'd meet at midnight - very romantic! And frustrating. In the cloudy ignorance of that high-minded yester-world we knew nothing of sexual relationship except that it be unspoken and forbidden to us. We wandered, snuggled tight, and concealed ourselves in a beach shelter.

The moon was in a perigee phase. It hung in a sky famished of all else, so bright I couldn't see beyond even to the stars. Anne first noticed the greying over.

'Sea mist,' I mumbled, replacing her hand on my thigh to encourage it upwards.

'No, look!'

She removed her hand, again, twisting my head to the south.

There was no mist. But overhead the radiated albedo of the moon retracted, as though some celestial breath blew across its face, gradually obscuring the orb itself.

Imagine a smoky room. The smoke expands and pans, it drifts and turns and snakes around, subduing the light. Now imagine the same, but no smoke. An undefined opaqueness drifting and quivering, lazily blurring and sharpening, gliding in and out of focus. It was like that. And eerily silent.

Suddenly Anne grabbed me, frozen, staring straight out to sea which also, through the shifting haze, was no longer visible.

But something else was. Moving towards us. Or rather, as the ghostly shapes slowly acquired density and form, *they* were moving towards us. The spectral creatures trudged up the beach and gathered around. Not invisible: we could see them. But not solid either. Sort of transparent? No, translucent. That's the word. Some sort of dinosaur. Huge great things, the largest as tall as a bungalow, in fact well over.

The first one lumbered past without noticing us. Great spikes down its back and a massive tail which draped behind, a bit like an elephant. But these were no elephants.

Much later, weeks later, I went to the library to look them up. When I saw the pictures, I knew. A Stegosaur. I lost count how of many in the herd. One, a youngster I guess, given its childish inquisitiveness, came up to investigate.

'It's so cute!' Anne now released me and stood, slowly so as not to frighten the beast, and held out her hand. And, I swear this is true, the calf leaned in to sniff her human scent.

'Don't!'

I thought her hand would go through the non-solid beast, but no. She rubbed her hand along its flank. She could touch it. Feel it.

'It's so cute!'

There was a metal rubbish bin. Three feet high? Bit more? Anne clambered up on to it and then up onto the calf's back. This was not real – but it was happening. Had our earth, our time, gone? Were we seeing back to a distant past? Or were we in it? Did these creatures perish in some cataclysmic event when the tides rose, ghosts from a herd long dead from catastrophe? It had happened many times in history.

The baby Steg quivered very gently as if to balance Anne's fragile weight, then it rejoined its shadowy comrades, forming in line along the footpath, plodding westward. I cowered in the shelter. Then the moon broke through. The sea came back. The dinosaur ghosts were instantly gone. As if aroused from deep sleep. I realised I was alone. I found her coat on the bench. I lost track of time.

The police car stopped when they saw me. They became very suspicious on finding Anne's coat, but no Anne. Then they awoke her parents, brought them down. And took me in for questioning. Several days I 'helped with their enquiries' while the search for Anne went on. Unsuccessfully.

No-one believed my story, but nor could they show otherwise. Fact was, there *were* dinosaur footprints along Littlehampton's seafront, for a mile and a half from that shelter to the lighthouse jetty, where they disappeared back into the water. Fact!

Eventually the police let me go. I moved away to avoid the stares and accusations. I was young, then. A kid. I am now old.

I have heard it said that as you age you remember yesterday better. And yes, I do. My dreams become daily more vivid. One day I will not wake up. Then I will meet Anne once more.

Wherever she is.

Note – Albert Roy was a journalist and now enjoys writing stories – we loved this one.

2

MOONLIGHT

Patricia Feinberg Stoner

For Purdey.

The little dog barked and wagged his tail hopefully, but no-one came. The river Arun flowed swift and turbulent under the full moon, swollen with the incoming tide, but here in the shelter of the Littlehampton marina all was calm; the boats bobbed peacefully at their moorings. The dog barked again and ran along the jetty in the moonlight, and cast no shadow.

Months passed, and years, and still at the full of the moon the little dog came and barked and trotted along the jetty in the moonlight, and cast no shadow.

And then one night a man came, stooped and ancient, and he moved painfully along the jetty. The dog barked and frisked and his tail was a blur of welcome. The man bent to stroke the dog, and when he rose he stood straight and tall. Together the man and dog walked along the boardwalk, in the moonlight, beside the sleeping boats, and cast no shadow.

A month passed, and two, and three. The man and the dog waited, but no-one came. At the seventh full moon a woman appeared at the jetty. She moved slowly, leaning on a stick, and the moonlight snagged in her sparse white hair. The man held out his arms and the dog jumped and twisted with joy. The woman embraced the man and bent to hug the dog, and when she rose she stood lithe and slender and her black hair cascaded down her back.

The man and the woman and the dog walked along the boardwalk in the moonlight, and cast no shadow. They reached the end of the jetty, where a trim blue and white boat sat, though in the light of the moon it was silver and black. The man got into the boat, and the dog jumped in, then the man gave his hand to the woman and she too stepped in to the tiny cockpit.

Noiselessly, the boat pulled away from its mooring and headed for the entrance to the marina. It turned downstream and sailed towards the river mouth and the sea beyond. And vanished in the moonlight.

Note - Patricia Feinberg Stoner is a member of CHINDI and leader of Arun Scribes. She writes books of comic verse and about France. Her books are available on Amazon.

3

RIVER OF DESTINY

Janet Edington

I'm not an imaginative sort of chap, not given to flights of fancy, but I know what I saw and Rosie saw it too. I'd taken her for her evening walk and we went down Terminus Road, past the Steam Packet and onto the footbridge. Rosie knew where we were going and was looking forward to a good run in the fields beyond. When we reached the centre of the bridge, we stopped.

It was a lovely evening; the clouds had vanished leaving the sky clear and translucent; all trace of sunset had faded and the sky was beginning to darken. Then I saw the faintest of sickle moons in the east as the sun sank towards the south west. The tide was also at its peak – a high spring tide.

There's something about a new moon that rouses deep emotion; no wonder folk used to see a witch on a broomstick riding in that heavenly swing. I stood for a long time looking at the river as it flowed steadily to the sea, then bent to stroke Rosie as she sat patiently at my side.

It was then that I felt it; the fur of her ruff was standing on end, yet I'd heard and seen nothing to account for her sudden wariness. That wariness ran up my arm and down my spine so that I too felt my body tingle with apprehension. The bridge was empty; no one had been on it when we began to cross and no one had entered it since we stopped, yet I knew there was someone behind us.

I can tell you that it took some courage to look behind me; I don't know what I expected to see but it certainly wasn't what I did see. I turned in time to catch a dark figure falling off the railings on the north side of the bridge. Those railings are very high because this is a known suicide spot; the river is second only to the River Severn when in full spate. I say *fell* because it was as if that body just slumped into the river; it didn't jump.

By now it was growing quite dark but the river seemed to collect all the light going and was a strip of liquid mercury. For a moment the dark figure was poised against that silvery mirror – then it disappeared. There was no splash; in fact there was no sound at all. Even the dull roar of traffic on the A259 road bridge was stilled and the gulls that usually make such a din had gone elsewhere.

And there was something else: it was as if the world around us had stopped when that body dropped from the footbridge; as if Rosie and I were trapped in a bubble of space from which time had been excluded. By now, we were at the northern rail looking down into the gleaming river. There was a dimple where something had entered the water and concentric rings of ripples to show the surface had indeed been disturbed. But there was no body – nothing.

I went to the south side to see if whatever-it-was had appeared from under the bridge but again there was nothing – merely a few ripples coming from upstream. For a long time Rosie and I looked at each other in puzzlement and amazement. What on earth had we seen? I didn't know and if Rosie did, she wasn't able to tell me. Well, there was no point in jumping into the freezing water to rescue an invisible jumper – if that is what we saw – so we decided to continue with our walk and return home to tell Margaret what we'd seen.

At that time, Margaret was deeply involved with a new craze: tracing her ancestors on the computer. She was Littlehampton born and bred but knew little about her forebears because her mother had died when she was ten and her father was a taciturn old curmudgeon who didn't answer questions on principle. So she was filling in gaps from her researches. We'd be lucky if she'd been able to drag herself away from the computer to prepare our dinner.

You can imagine how eager I was to tell my wife about the strange happening on the bridge, but I wasn't able to get a word in edgeways because she was jumping up and down with excitement and grabbed my arm the moment we arrived.

'Alfred, you remember what I'd found out about Mum's granddad – that he was illegitimate and brought up by his grandmother not his mother? Well, I now know why. I've just read an article from the local paper dated 8th December 1867; it reports the death of Rosemary Brown (commonly known as Rosie) who jumped into the river on the evening of the fourth, ten days after giving birth to a baby boy. She was only fifteen years old. What do you think of that, Alfred?'

'Do you realise what the date is, Margie?'

'No, and what has that got to do with anything? It's not your birthday or our wedding anniversary; that I do know.'

'It's December the fourth 2017; precisely one hundred and fifty years to the day since your great, great grandmother jumped into the Arun. What do you think of that, my dear?'

Then I told her what Rosie and I had seen.

Note – Janet Edington is a member of the The Nook writing group in Rustington.

4

THE GHOST OF OYSTER POND

Philippa Bower

Did you hear about Alicia Bond
Who drowned herself in the Oyster Pond?
At dead of night when the moon is high
By the Oyster Pond you can hear a sigh
And a breeze although the air is still
And suddenly feel a ghostly chill.
A misty shadow will then appear
And a terrible scream will rend the air.
Is it the scream of Alicia Bond?
No, it's you who scream by the Oyster Pond.

Note – Philippa Bower runs the U3A writing group in Arun East.

5

THE HARBOUR CAT

Teresa Harrison-Best

No one really knew where the cat came from, or whether he had a story to tell. He just sort of appeared out of thin air. He showed up with several war wounds including a kink in his stripy tail.

The fishermen quite liked having him around as he kept the rodents down to the minimum; they rewarded him richly with small pieces of fish and the odd prawn. Life for the little cat was pretty good so he stuck around.

Everyone took to calling him Mr Sea (a very strange attempt at humour you may think, but they were fishermen, not poets). Some of the men thought about taking him in, but he preferred life on the harbour instead. On bad weather nights he would take refuge in the lifeboat house; the crew didn't mind, as he was becoming a regular friendly face there as well.

All the local children were very fond of Mr Sea; he would rub up against them and purr, which gave them a fit of the giggles. All the locals knew him as the harbour cat and he became a regular sight on the waterfront. He enjoyed a little tickle under the chin and regular strokes.

Everything was fair and dandy until the old harbour master retired back in 1820. A little weasel of a man called Lionel Stropp replaced him and things began to change for Mr Sea, but not for the good. Stroppy, as he was nicknamed, insisted that the cat was to be got rid of. He hated cats with a passion. The fishermen tried to conceal Mr Sea every time they knew Stropp was visiting the harbour. Mr Sea, though, had other ideas and continued to strut along the promenade as though he owned it.

One day, Stropp was so incensed when he saw the little cat that he kicked Mr Sea off the harbour wall into the freezing water. All that the fishermen heard was a small splash. Several days passed and there was no sign of Mr Sea, and everyone, except Mr Stropp, was worried about the little cat.

It was one of the old fishermen who overheard Lionel Stropp boasting to his assistant that he had kicked the cat into the water, and that the cat had perished. Soon after that, Lionel Stropp's life took a severe nosedive: his wife packed her bags and left him because of his cruelty. His heavy drinking led him to be dismissed from his job and, as a result, he lost his tied cottage. Lionel Stropp was now a desperately unhappy man.

After his dismissal, and several weeks later, as the harbour was slowly returning to normal, the community heard that Lionel Stropp had fatally shot himself.

The replacement harbour master was a kindly man whom everybody seemed to like. He would pass the time of day with the fishermen and those walking the riverbank alike. A few years had passed when, one day, he mentioned to one of the older fishermen that he had been talking to a little cat preening himself by the water's edge. He explained that the cat had a kinked stripy tail and seemed very wet, as though he had fallen into water. The fisherman asked the harbour master to describe the cat in more detail and soon learned that the cat he was describing was exactly like Mr Sea. That's impossible, he thought: Mr Sea drowned many years ago.

Even to this day there are occasional sightings of a small cat with a kinked, stripy tail sitting on the harbour wall, or by the water's edge, preening himself. It's rumoured that many people have taken photographs of the little wet cat, but when they check later there's no cat in the picture. Some people reported that they even tried to approach the cat to stroke him but that he suddenly vanished.

So, next time you visit Littlehampton harbour look out for a little cat with a stripy, kinked tail ... he may be sitting on the wall preening himself.

Note - Teresa Harrison-Best is a member of Scribblers Writers in Littlehampton.

6

BINGO

Carol Thomas

When my sister and I were little, Friday night meant going to bingo with our mum. I was seven, and my sister was ten. We found it an adventure, and we knew that if we behaved, at the end of the night we would get a bar of fudge. It was worth it.

Mum played bingo at the Regal Bingo Club, in the centre of town. It was a big building, flanked by shops on either side. Inside it was built like a theatre. The auditorium seemed large, and I remember there was a bar.

Back then mum was a smoker, so we sat upstairs. The wall of the stairwell was damp and had patches of peeling paint. Even at my age, I could tell the place had seen better days. There was a heavy curtain that was pulled across when the bingo was on. The balcony only hid a few rows of the stalls so from our vantage point, in the circle, we could see the people below.

We sat on the itchy seats that always felt like they might tip and swallow me up and listened to the numbers being called. The first game always seemed the longest because after that we were given Mum's used bingo cards and a pen, so we could pretend to play along. If we got bored, we were allowed to play hide and seek. We were the only children there, so as long as we were quiet, nobody minded. Mum let us go round the back rows of seats and as far as the stairwell. It was fun, until that last time.

We had been playing for a while. My sister was better at hiding than me, she didn't mind crawling into the dark spaces under the seats, and she never got scared the way I did. When it was my turn to hide, I imagined I could hear breathing next to me or that I could feel something touching me. My sister teased me about it, sometimes making me jump on purpose.

I remember, that last time we went to bingo, I sat on the top step counting. As I reached ten I opened my eyes, and let them readjust to the light before whispering, 'Coming, ready or not.' That's when I heard her call from the shadows at the bottom of the stairwell.

'Come and find me.'

But as I was about to run down the stairs, in the direction of the voice, my sister appeared from the curtain behind me. She looked pale, and her eyes were wide. She grabbed me and pulled me into her arms. I could feel her heart thudding as she held me close and gasped, 'Don't go, I heard that too.'

From 1936 to 1967 the Odeon cinema stood proudly in the middle of Littlehampton town centre. In 1967 it was sold by Rank to Classic cinemas. While it remained a cinema, bingo was introduced on a part-time basis. In 1974 the last film was shown, and the Regal Bingo Club opened its doors.

The Regal Bingo Club was demolished in 1984. It was where Costa Coffee is now.

Note – Carol Thomas is a member of CHINDI and writes romantic novels and children's books. Find them on Amazon.

7

LITTLEHAMPTON LILY

Maureen Wells

Just after five that morning, a lone, timid fox loped about in search of sustenance.

Karen hurried along South Terrace towards Beach Road. Yesterday in the arcade she'd spotted a figure in white running ahead of her, calling a man's name. She heard no footsteps. The town centre was empty save for a few rough sleepers in dilapidated cardboard boxes. Shadows danced like skeleton figures. Was someone lurking, ready to pounce from a doorway?

Her heart pounding, she tried to banish her fears of the dark. She needed this new job cleaning trains. Her partner had dumped her, and she had debts.

Arriving in Terminus Road, she approached Littlehampton station. Changing into overalls and donning rubber gloves, she started working at the front of a London train, collecting crisp packets, crumpled cans, used tissues and soiled nappies.

Soon this station would become part of the hustle and bustle of Littlehampton and the thought lessened her isolation. Reaching the end carriage, she realised she wasn't alone. A woman in a white dress sat, her head turned towards the window. There was no face in the reflection. Karen wanted to run across to the train where her colleague, Ben, was working but she froze, her mouth dry. Was this the same woman as yesterday?

'You shouldn't be on this train,' she stuttered. 'It's not in service yet.'

No reply. Was it merely her imagination? Then she heard mournful murmurings.

Karen groped for her phone. She'd ask for Ben's help. Little matter that her co-worker resented her getting this job, instead of his friend.

No answer. She left a message, all the while wondering about the faceless woman; how she'd arrived on the train and who had forgotten to lock the doors.

'I need to clean this train. You have to get off,' Karen called out.

Still no reply. She crept further down the aisle but when she approached the last seats, no-one was there. She started to shake, fearing she was going mad, hoping it was a trick of the light.

Over on the adjoining platform Ben was having an illicit smoke and she hurried over.

'I'm coming,' he muttered. 'What's up?' He stubbed out his cigarette.

'Nothing,' she said, trying to sound casual. 'Just thought I heard someone in the train.'

'Rats probably. They're everywhere.' He walked off, leaving Karen slightly reassured. She tried to push away the episode, despite her doubts about eerie sounds and the mysterious woman.

Next day she followed the same route and as she entered the arcade, she caught sight of a woman in a full-skirted white dress. Fear filled her, but she had to continue to work. The mortgage payment was now overdue.

She recognised the early morning shopkeeper when he called, 'You alright, love?'

'Did you see a woman in white hurrying towards the station?'

'Not you as well,' he chuckled. 'That's our Littlehampton Lily. I've never seen her but others have, though not her face. She's searching for her fiancé who never returned from war.'

'So, she's still alive?'

'Gracious no! Poor Lily died of a broken heart years ago.'

'But I saw her. On the train.'

'Means you've got special powers. Don't worry, Lily can't hurt you. She's still wearing her wedding dress and searching for her groom.'

Karen clocked in at the station. There was no sign of Ben, but she wasn't afraid now. If she saw Lily, she'd let her know she understood her torment.

For sisterhood lives on in Littlehampton.

Note – Maureen Wells runs The Nook writing group in Rustington.

8

SUPERMARKET CHALLENGE

Angela Petch

On nights when the moon is in its shroud and the tide leaches from the ship's hull where I lie, I slip from my muddy bed, drift along the quay, past shops and silent houses along Pier Road to the old timber yard. It's flattened now, beneath where the supermarket squats ugly, its blue and yellow signs faint in the gloom. Where once upon a time I breathed in honey resin and heard the whine of saws, now freezers hum; their bellies filled with ostrich steaks and German strudels. I protested in life at the rape of my home and now my restless spirit makes mischief. My need to be heard pulls me from the rotting timbers that reach up like arms begging to be released.

This morning, I tarried longer, curling my shape between the ceiling ducts of the store to watch the effects of my mayhem.

'Oh – my – God!' The woman called Dawn stopped half way down the aisle of Lidl with her tray of aubergines. Oil, broken glass and sundried tomatoes lay scattered and splashed like a murder scene. 'That shelf's bloody collapsed *again.*'

Young Shannayah approached from round a freezer. 'Jeez – what the …? I watched Nitin fix that yesterday with his big drill.'

'Yeah, right, that's not all you were watching, Shann,' Dawn muttered.

'I can't help it if he's got a nice bum.'

'Go and fetch the mop and tell the boss we've had another incident,' Dawn said as she tiptoed through the debris.

Half an hour later, over their snatched coffee-break, I eavesdropped on Iwona and Dawn. In the past weeks, they had wondered how boxes of toothpaste had inexplicably turned up in the fish freezer, bottles of vodka amongst baby products, loo rolls under pineapples.

'Maybe the shelf broke because – what you call it – this is earthmoving area?' Iwona suggested. New from Poland, she was still mastering English.

'Ha! Not much earthmoving going on round here,' Dawn sniggered.

'Please?'

'I think you mean earthquake.'

Then the manager pushed open the door. 'Speed it up, ladies,' he said. 'Delivery arrives in five ...'

'Stan, you are a slave-driver,' Dawn said, dunking her doughnut. 'We've only just finished clearing up that mess.'

'I need to talk to everybody about that. I want a volunteer to keep watch through the night. Whoever's having a laugh needs to stop.'

I hung around Lidl all day and smiled when I heard complaints of strange smells and chills. I heard Shannayah volunteer to share the night shift with Nitin, but he said it was against his religion. When everyone had left, he arranged his sleeping bag in the corner of Stan's office and started a game on his iPad. The door was ajar and the hum of freezers and gentle patter of rain on the roof must have been soothing, because he fell asleep. A tap on the window made him jump.

'Let me in, son,' called a voice, 'your mother has sent more supplies.'

His father was wrapped against the cold sea wind. 'Mum's sent some Chicken Madras and Granny sent you her walking stick. In case of intruders.'

They laughed and after reassuring his Dad he was fine, Nitin locked up and returned to the office to enjoy his midnight feast.

I decided to spook him.

Glass shattered as a top shelf of spirits collapsed onto the tiles. Nitin emerged from the office with his Granny's walking stick. He reached for a bottle of cider and flung it at me. His missile passed straight through my shadow and hit the shelf below the spirits - Cabernet Sauvignon and Merlot tumbled like skittles in a bowling alley. He flung a couple of cans and they passed through me too. He ran home screaming like a banshee and I suppose he hid under his duvet and passed a sleepless night.

When Nitin dawdled into work next morning, three police cars, blue lights flashing, were parked outside Lidl and the entrance was cordoned off. Shannayah fell into his arms, hot tears and mascara soaking his shirt front. She looked up at him through smeared panda eyes and sobbed. 'I warned everybody. I told them there was something weird about this place – just like in the Exorcist ... and now it's gone and happened.' She sobbed some more. 'Stan's dead. Dawn found him under a new delivery of dogfood ...

squashed … blood everywhere … bottles smashed …' Nitin pulled her into an awkward embrace.

From my vantage point above the bread ovens, I smirked. Maybe the penny was beginning to drop with these numpties. I will continue to nail my message home and inflict revenge. Until they find my bones and lay me properly to rest, I will make more mischief.

Note – Angela Petch is a member of CHINDI and Arun Scribes. She writes historical novels which can be found on Amazon and has several short stories published in women's magazines.

9

A HALLOWEEN STORY

Maggie Brown

It was cold that Halloween and a sea mist rolled in towards evening, obscuring everything. My friend Emily and I were walking into town clutching hold of each other, giggling about the Halloween party we were going to at the Dolphin Hotel. Our friends were wearing fancy dress and we didn't want to be outdone so we both wore long gothic style dresses, high heels and pinned-up hair under black and gold hats. I thought we looked very good, striking in fact: willowy Emily with her blonde hair; me shorter, darker.

Rounding a corner Emily grabbed my arm. 'Nadine' she said. 'Can you see that funny chap on the bench? Don't like the look of him.' We paused, glimpsing a strange man in fancy dress, shrouded in sea mist, peering through the fog. He wore a wide black hat and what looked like a long coat and breeches down to his knees. Hearing the clickety clack of our footsteps, he stood up, looking straight at us.

'Well, my pretty maidens, where are you going on this dreadful night?' he said, in a heavily accented voice. I thought he was getting into party mode and answered back in a similar vein.

'Sir, we are on our way to a special party. Have you had an invitation?'

'No', he said. 'I'm looking for a particular inn reputed to be in this town. I've been trying to find it ever since my ship went down. I come every year on this date hoping someone will direct me.'

We looked at each other in confusion. Why was he talking like that? Unease crept up my spine. We tried to ignore him and hurry on to the pub, but he blocked our way.

'In just such a fog as this we collided offshore with another ship. It was every man for himself, but I called out to my shipmates that if they made it to land we should meet at the Dolphin, in town. If you young wenches could direct me I would be much obliged.'

Emily clutched at my hand in terror. Together we turned, hitched up our long skirts and fled back the way we had come. I glanced over my shoulder to make sure we weren't being followed, but all I saw was the seat veiled in mist. Emily and I carried on to the Dolphin via another route. As the fog swirled around, I still felt the presence of another person but couldn't hear footsteps. At last we arrived, I pushed open the door leaving behind the cold, ethereal mist whirling about our heads. It was great to see our college friends already there.

'Hey!' one of them shouted, 'Close the door quick, you're bringing in that sea fog.'

Shutting the door, we put aside our fear to enjoy the Halloween evening with great music, ghostly jokes and spooky tricks all played by a local DJ. Towards the end of the evening, after numerous drinks, I described the encounter with the stranger to a couple of boys from college who clearly didn't believe me.

'Oh my God, Nadine, you two must have been hitting the bottle and seeing things before you even got here,' said one of them. 'Are you sure it wasn't a trick or treat?'

'No, honestly, we didn't have time for a drink before we set out.' I said.

I put the odd experience out of my mind and the celebrations went on until late in the night.

The next day I wondered whether to mention the stranger to my parents or the police. Whilst debating what to do, I decided to google shipwrecks off the coast of Littlehampton. Staring at the screen, I read that two ships had collided in the fog over a hundred years ago. One had been a passenger steamer from Liverpool and the other a cargo ship sailing between Sardinia and Antwerp. My imagination worked overtime – what if the ghostly apparition were a drowned sailor still seeking his shipmates?

Note – Maggie Brown is a member of Arun East U3A writing group.

10

MAUD GRAY

Annette Brampton

In 1918 the SS Shirala, a cargo ship with over 200 passengers, set sail from London on its way to Bombay, India. Just a few miles off the coast of Littlehampton, it sank. A German 'U' boat in the vicinity was thought to be responsible. Local fishermen rallied to rescue the crew and passengers. Most were grateful to be plucked from the raging sea. One passenger alone, Maud Gray, was not happy. This is her story:

The ship listed, people sliding towards the edge, some falling straight overboard into the murky waters. People screaming, total panic around me. I had never been so frightened. Was this it? Would our baby Anna never get to meet her father? Were we going to die? The ship was sinking, and there was no going back. I clutched Anna to me, wrapping her close with my long scarf, tightening the knots until I felt we were one. Anna was wide eyed and had stopped crying. She just stared up at me with such trust.

Then I saw some passengers I knew.

'Boats are coming, Maud,' they were shouting.

I saw lights in the distance. The ship groaned again and began to roll.

'Jump, Maud!' they screamed. 'It's our only hope.'

So I did! I did! Anna and I crashed into the freezing water and I kicked us to the surface. We coughed and spluttered. Her little body wriggled against me, but she was tight against my chest. I kicked towards the boats, but then I felt my scarf loosen and Anna slipped away. My baby! I saw her little face once more before a wave overwhelmed her and she was lost! I'm not a strong swimmer but I dived and swam, searching, calling for her, shrieking her name! Suddenly, I felt strong arms around me, hauling me into a boat.

'No!' I cried, twisting, pleading. 'Please, my baby's in the water. Please!'

The fisherman wrestled with me and pulled me back into the boat, refusing to let me go. They wrapped me in warm blankets while they searched for Anna in the rough waters. Too soon, they gave up and headed for the shore.

Such was my despair that I wailed and screamed and the whole boat cried with me.

Once ashore, a kind fisherman led me to The Nelson where his cousin was the landlady. She made me welcome and gave me a bed, in return for cleaning and serving behind the bar while the authorities tried to contact my husband in Bombay.

My heart broken; my grief endless. I did as I was asked, and in my spare time wandered the harbour, beseeching the fishermen to bring Anna back to me. They began to avoid me, their eyes telling me there was no hope. Instead I began to wander by the boating lake. Sometimes I glimpsed a fish or two, as the seagulls whirled above. I began to feed the gulls scraps, willing them to become my friends as they flocked to my side. They were gentle with me, their beady eyes observing my sorrow. Perhaps they understood me as I pleaded with them to search for my baby. I flung the bread high, raising my arms to them crying out to them to find my Anna. And they flew off over the sea searching and screeching her name. 'Anna, Anna'.

People began to stop and point at me. Did they think me mad, the way I talked to the birds? Days, weeks and months passed with no word from my husband. Was he too lost in the war? Maybe his spirit was with Anna. Time lost meaning, only a blur. Although people were very kind to me, my only solace came from my friends, the gulls. Join us, they screeched, join us Maud, join our search for Anna.

Poor Maud drowned in the shallow waters of the boating lake one morning. A fisherman found her face down in the water and raised the alarm. He had been drawn to the lake by the unusual mass of gulls screeching and flapping around the pond.

In the summer months, in the very early hours of the day, people have seen the eerie figure of a young woman dressed in a long black mourning dress of the time, wandering by the pond. Always she is seen staring upwards and reaching out with her arms. Reports say she is surrounded by seagulls. If you listen carefully to the gulls, maybe you can hear them screeching the name Anna, just as Maud did.

Note - Annette Brampton is a member of Quills Writing Group at Worthing Library.

11

FLYERS

Rosemary Noble

Imagine, if you will, a foggy night around ten o'clock late in 1941. A middle-aged woman alights from the last train from London. She's weary after an arduous, tiring journey from a northern town. Remember it's the blackout era, and she's a stranger. She asks the porter for directions to a hotel and he points her to the two hotels over the road towards the right. She fumbles in her bag for a tip, but he waves away her hand and she thanks him for his kindness. Taking a pocket torch from her bag she begins her lonely walk. First, she calls in at The Steam Packet, but is soon turned away; next it's the Arun View, but the same thing happens. They recommend she retrace her steps towards the town centre. Back she trudges, shivering in the cool sea mist and desperate for a cup of something warm, but her thermos is empty. It seems a long time since the tea stand at Victoria Station. The Norfolk Hotel suggest she try The Dolphin which in turn suggest she try The Crown. So many hotels, so little room.

She can hardly bear to go on any longer. *Please*, she prays, *please someone take pity on me*, as she walks through the blackout curtain of the Crown. She makes her way to the reception desk and dings the bell on the counter. A woman peers from a back office.

'We're full, there's no rooms vacant, if that's what you're looking for.'

'Can you at least find me a hot drink?' Sylvia begs, weariness evident in her voice. The woman nods and turns in the direction of the kitchen. A man appears from the same office. He looks sympathetically at her.

'I've tried everywhere else, no one has a room,' she replied to his unspoken question.

'If you go in the lounge bar,' he points towards a door, 'I'll bring you some cushions and blankets and you can sleep there.' She would agree to anything and feels like hugging him but turns towards the door and finding the room empty, sinks on to a hard chair and kicks off her shoes. After sipping a cup of unsweetened, weak tea, she arranges and then curls up in the motley pile of cushions and blankets and closes her eyes, falling fast asleep.

Next morning, after freshening herself up, she stands at the desk to pay the bill. The landlord smiles at her.

'Did you sleep?'

'For the first time in days. Thank you for letting me stay. I wondered why you offered me room to stay, when everywhere else turned me down.'

'It was those two airmen beside you, nodding to me. How could I turn down the mother of those brave pilots? In the Blitz we saw them every day, up in the air, dog-fighting with the Jerries. We're so proud of those boys.'

Sylvia catches her breath, unable to speak, she nods and turns, hot tears spilling down her cheeks. The telegram from 23 Squadron Leader at Ford burns a hole in her pocket, 'Regret to inform you, missing in action, both of your sons.'

Note – Rosemary is a member of CHINDI and Arun Scribes. Her published books are available on Amazon and from bookshops.

Printed in Great Britain
by Amazon

58881524R00030